Little Bears go on a Picnic

Heather Maisner

Illustrated by
Tomislav Zlatic

W
FRANKLIN WATTS
LONDON • SYDNEY

Hello. I'm Big Bear. Today I'm taking the little bears for a picnic by the lake.

But they are so excited, they can't keep still. They keep knocking things over and playing hide-and-seek. Can you help me, please?

Harry

Olivia

Jack

Lily

Evie

Kitchen towels

Cereals

Water

Bread

Muffins

Bread rolls

Eggs

We're at the supermarket. The little bears have moved some things around. Can you spot which things are in the wrong places? Where do they belong?

Lettuce

Tomatoes

Pears

Grapes

Potatoes

Pram

Now we're in the park. The little bears have been running about and everyone is confused. Can you please put everything back in its proper place?

Helmet

Duck

Football

Dog

Hat

Sheep

Goose

Chicken

I asked the little bears to go quietly through the farm but they simply ran wild. Can you please put these animals and objects back where they belong?

Cow

Hay

Wheel

Mask

Ball

Cup

Goodness me! There's a funfair on
the playing field. The little bears
went crashing through and have
knocked things all over the place.
Do please help me to tidy up.

Balloon

Saddle

Steering
wheel

Paper plate

Deckchair

Banana

Now we're at the lake. The little bears began to set out the picnic but then ran away to play, leaving a mess.

Towel

Crisps

Can you help me tidy up, please?

It's time to walk home now. But I can't carry all these towels. Can you please give each little bear the correct towel. And hand them each their own backpack, too.

Thank you. I hoped to read the
newspaper when I got home
but now I can't find it. Can you
see it anywhere?

What a very exciting time we've had! Now everything has been put away and at last I can sit down and read. Do please come and visit us again.

More from the Little Bears!

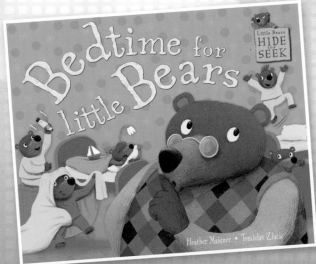

Bedtime for little Bears

Heather Maisner • Tomislav Zlatic

978 1 4451 4323 1

Little Bears go to School

Heather Maisner • Tomislav Zlatic

978 1 4451 4327 9

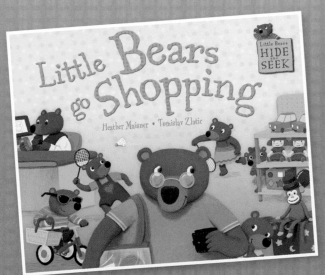

Little Bears go Shopping

Heather Maisner • Tomislav Zlatic

978 1 4451 4325 5

Franklin Watts
Published in paperback in Great Britain in 2019 by The Watts Publishing Group

Text copyright © Heather Maisner 2016
Illustrations © Tomislav Zlatic 2016

Series Editor: Sarah Peutrill
Cover Designer: Cathryn Gilbert
ISBN: 978 1 4451 4329 3

Printed in China

Franklin Watts
An imprint of
Hachette Children's Group
Part of The Watts Publishing Group
Carmelite House
50 Victoria Embankment
London EC4Y 0DZ

An Hachette UK Company
www.hachette.co.uk

www.franklinwatts.co.uk

FSC
www.fsc.org

MIX
Paper from responsible sources
FSC® C104740